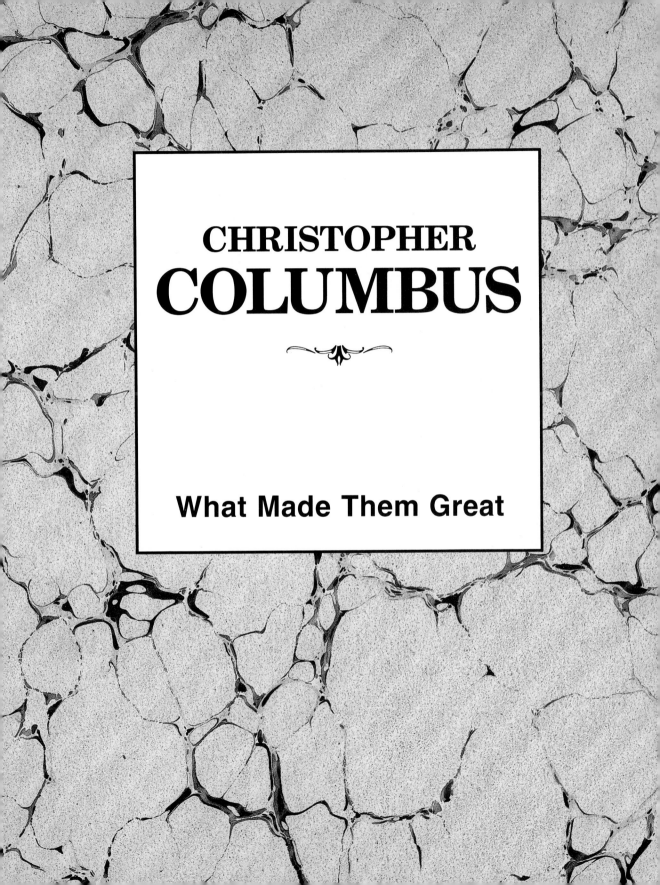

CHRISTOPHER
COLUMBUS

What Made Them Great

CHRISTOPHER COLUMBUS

What Made Them Great

Lee Morgan

Illustrated by Claudio Solarino

SILVER BURDETT PRESS

ACKNOWLEDGMENTS

We would like to thank Professor J.K. Sowards, Department of History, Wichita State University; David A. Williams, Professor Emeritus, Department of History, California State University, Long Beach; and Craighton Hippenhammer, Cuyahoga County Public Library, Ohio for their guidance and helpful suggestions.

Project Editor: Emily Easton (Silver Burdett Press)

Adapted and reformatted from the original by Kirchoff/Wohlberg, Inc.

Project Director: John R. Whitman
Graphics Coordinator: Jessica A. Kirchoff
Production Coordinator: Marianne Hile

Library of Congress Cataloging-in-Publication Data

Morgan, Lee, 1934—
    Christopher Columbus/Lee Morgan; illustrated by Claudio Solarino.
    p. cm.—[FROM SERIES: What Made Them Great]

Adaptation of: Christopher Columbo/Lino Monchieri; translated by Mary Lee Grisanti.
    © 1985 Silver Burdett Company, Morristown, New Jersey.
    [FROM SERIES: Why They Became Famous]
    Includes bibliographical references.
Summary: An account of Columbus's four transatlantic voyages.
1. Columbus, Christopher—Juvenile literature. 2. Explorers—America—Biography—
    Juvenile literature. 3. Explorers—Spain—Biography—Juvenile literature. [1. Columbus,
    Christopher. 2. Explorers. 3. America—Discovery and exploration—Spanish.] I. Solarino,
    Claudio, ill. II. Monchieri, Lino. Perché Sono Diventati Famoso, Colombo. III. Series.

E111.M855 1990   970.01'5—dc20   [B]   [92]   89-38849   CIP   AC

© Fabbri Editori S.p.A., Milan 1982
Translated into English by Mary Lee Grisanti for Silver Burdett Press
from Perché Sono Diventati Famosi: Colombo
First published in Italy in 1982 by Fabbri Editori S.p.A., Milan

10 9 8 7 6 5 4 3 2 1 (Library Binding)
10 9 8 7 6 5 4 3 2 1 (Softcover)

ISBN 0-382-09974-5 (Library Binding)
ISBN 0-382-24001-4 (Softcover)

TABLE OF CONTENTS

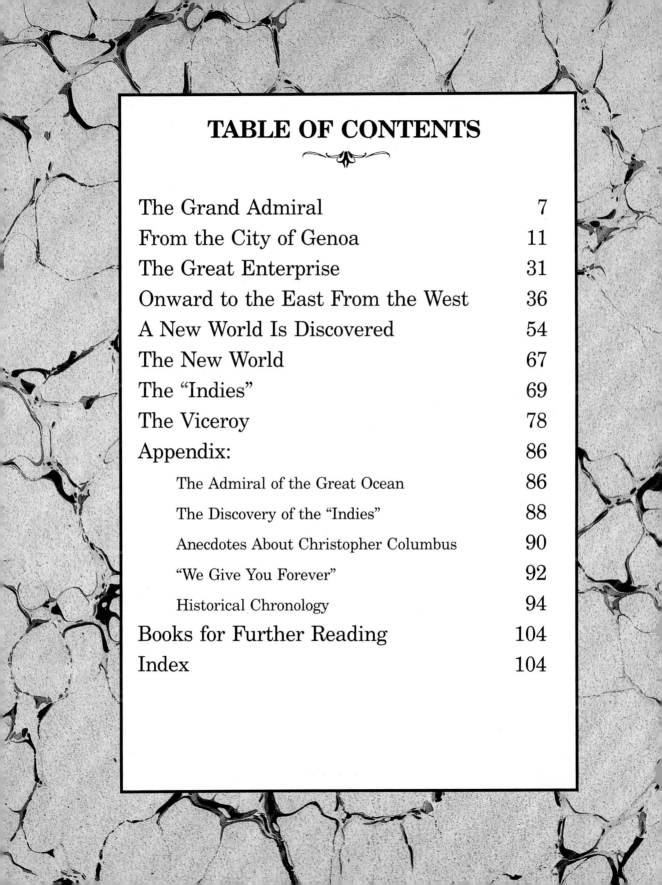

The Grand Admiral

The sky was blue. Trumpets blew and drums sounded. Suddenly the huge crowd fell silent. It seemed almost as if an unseen hand was reaching down to hush their voices.

It was a bright April day in the year 1493. The people of Barcelona jammed the streets of the city. They gathered to watch an important moment. Such an event had never happened before in the history of Spain. Indeed, nothing like this had ever taken place in the entire history of the world.

Through the tree-shaped square, a parade came slowly into sight. The banners of Aragon and Castile danced in the breeze. These two regions of Spain were now united under the rule of King Ferdinand and Queen Isabella.

Among the marchers were officials of the government and other people of importance. To celebrate this great occasion, everyone wore splendid robes. With them walked Christopher Columbus. People were now calling him admiral of the Great Ocean. But he had been given other grand titles as well—governor of the islands and viceroy of the king.

Behind Columbus walked a band of unusual men. The crowds stared in amazement. These men had skin the color of copper. They were clad in strange costumes decorated with feathers and gold.

They carried cages full of squawking parrots. For the first time, Europeans were seeing Native Americans.

Columbus had returned from a great voyage of discovery. He had brought these men home with him. Columbus believed he had reached the East Indies near China and Japan. So it was natural to call the copper-skinned men "Indians." In years to come, his mistake would become obvious. But from habit, people continue to use the word "Indian."

A few weeks earlier, Columbus and his men had landed at Palos, on the coast of Spain. From there he had immediately sent a letter to Isabella and Ferdinand. He asked to be received at court. He wished to tell the queen and king about his voyage. Permission was granted at once.

Throughout Barcelona, news of Columbus's return had spread rapidly. By the time he arrived, there was tremendous excitement.

This April day, the people of the city were in a festive mood. When they spied Columbus, the cheering began. The streets rang with shouts of "Long live the admiral!"

At the royal palace, the parade came to a halt. King Ferdinand and Queen Isabella were sitting on their thrones. Usually they kept their seats when greeting subjects. But today they rose to their feet. The king and queen wished to show their respect for Columbus's achievement. Like everyone else, they felt overcome with pride.

Columbus knelt to kiss their hands. Sitting beside the king and queen, he was eager to answer all of their questions. He told them about the exciting voyage across the Atlantic Ocean. He described the amazing lands he had discovered and the friendly people he had met.

Finally Columbus turned to the Indians. He called them to come forward. The king and queen stared at the handsome copper-skinned men. The Indians were startling proof that Columbus had visited distant lands.

The meeting ended. Then everyone went to the royal chapel. There was a special service to give thanks. The sailors had returned safely from their wonderful voyage. Leaving the chapel, Columbus was again hailed loudly.

The reception pleased Columbus. But he could not help looking back. Reaching the Far East by sailing west had been his lifelong dream. Most people had not believed it was possible. His problems had been crushing. Over and over his hopes had been dashed. At one point, he had even become so discouraged that he thought of leaving Spain. He had thought that perhaps the king of France might look on his plan with more favor than the Spanish.

But now, all of that lay behind him. He had sailed boldly out into the Atlantic. Now everyone knew he had been right. This beautiful spring day was his moment of glory.

From the City of Genoa

"I'm from the City of Genoa," Christopher Columbus always liked to say.

In northern Italy, Genoa faced the Mediterranean Sea. Rich and bustling, it was the most important seaport on the northwest coast. People who lived in Genoa were extremely proud of their home. They did not mind boasting and even called the city "Genoa the Proud."

In those days, ships from Genoa went forth to every part of the known world. Often the Italian ships crossed the Mediterranean to North Africa. In the African cities of Tunis and Tripoli, a great variety of goods were bought and sold.

At the same time, foreign vessels were constantly visiting Genoa. Along the wharves could be seen tall ships flying the flags of many lands. As Columbus was growing up, he was surrounded by ships and sailors.

Columbus was born in Genoa in 1451. But the exact day and month is not known. Not only a seaport, Genoa was also an important center for weaving. The whole Columbus family worked at turning sheep's wool into cloth. Christopher's parents were weavers.

Besides Christopher, there were several other children. Two of the boys were named Bartholomew and Giacomo. It must have been a close family. Years later, Christopher brought his two brothers to the New World. He felt pleased to have their help.

Christopher Columbus grew up to be a tall boy. He had broad shoulders. His hair was red. Freckles dusted his cheeks. A religious youth, he went to church often.

But he did not attend school. Nearly everything he learned from books he found out for himself.

It is not surprising that Columbus felt eager to go to sea. As a teenager, he first worked on ships that made short trips. Usually they carried wool and cloth to nearby ports in Italy and France.

Eventually, he began to go on longer voyages. One of these took him to Tunis. On another early voyage, he visited the Greek island of Chios.

Columbus's family probably expected him to become a weaver, like his father. By this time, however, he had made a decision. The cloth business did not appeal to him. Instead, he wanted to earn his living as a sailor.

The sight of tall wooden sailing ships rocking at anchor in the harbor thrilled him. The open sea seemed to call out.

"I love the taste of salt spray in my face," he once told a friend. "It's wonderful to feel the deck rising and falling under my feet."

Columbus was eager for adventure. Like many young men, he dreamed of seeing the world. When he was about twenty-five, he got his first glimpse of the Atlantic Ocean. This immense body of water washed the coastline of Europe. It extended as far as the eye could see. Over the edge of the horizon, the ocean rolled westward into the unknown. No European sailor had ever traveled far beyond that Western horizon.

The mysterious Atlantic always fascinated Columbus. In 1476, he shipped out with a fleet of trading ships. Part of the cargo was going to Portugal. Then the fleet was supposed to head north to England and Flanders (today, a part of Belgium). Leaving Genoa, the fleet steered toward the western end of the Mediterranean. At the Strait of Gibraltar, it passed through the Pillars of Hercules. Then the fleet edged its way out into the Atlantic.

In Europe at that time, war was raging. French ships prowled the ocean. Suddenly the Genoese fleet found itself under attack. They were helpless. Cannons began to crackle. Columbus was wounded. Several of the trading ships began to fill with water. Slowly they sank.

Before Columbus knew what was happening, he was thrown into the water. His ship was gone, sunk to the bottom of the ocean. He noticed an oar floating on the waves. Grabbing it quickly, he held on for his life.

Finally, he began to swim toward land. It was difficult because of his injuries. Many times the huge waves almost sucked him under. Amazingly, he somehow managed to swim six miles. He was exhausted when he washed up on the coast of Portugal.

In the fifteenth century, Portugal had the finest navy in the world. Its ships were the swiftest and most modern. Sailors came from all over Europe just to sail aboard Portuguese vessels. For Columbus, the shipwreck was bad luck. But ending up in Portugal was a piece of good luck. He decided to make the most of the opportunity. Why not stay in Portugal? Maybe he could make his fortune there.

The following year he sailed with a Portuguese trading fleet. Heading north, it first stopped at Galway on the coast of Ireland. Then it continued farther north to Iceland. Years later, people would remember this voyage of Columbus's. In Iceland, they said, Columbus heard stories about Leif Erikson and his Vikings.

Around 1000, the Vikings left Norway. They sailed across the Atlantic and landed in North America. This was probably northern Newfoundland. The Vikings named the place "Vinland."

But the story about Columbus and the Vikings must be wrong. Never once did he mention their voyage. Later on, he would insist that crossing the

Atlantic was a sensible plan. But he never said, "Remember how the Vikings crossed the sea? I can do it, too." It seems obvious that he had never heard of Erikson's travels.

Not long after his return from Iceland, Columbus married. His wife's name was Filipa Perestrello. She was Portuguese. They had a son called Diego. For a while they lived in the Madeira Islands off the coast of North Africa. Filipa's brother was the governor. At other times, the family lived in Lisbon.

Columbus continued going to sea. He became very successful. Within five years he was captain of a trading ship. Many of his voyages took him to the Gold Coast of West Africa.

At this time, Africa was still a mystery. Nobody knew for sure how far south the continent extended. Some geographers believed it ran right down to the South Pole. So Portuguese sea captains were very eager to explore the coast of Africa. However, Columbus was looking in a different direction.

His dream of voyaging across the Atlantic may have first occurred to him as a boy. In Genoa, he must have heard stories from many sailors. A curious lad, he surely asked questions. How is a sail unfurled? How do you steer with a compass? What happens when a storm blows up? The tales of seafaring men might very well have planted the idea in his mind.

While living in the Madeira Islands, Columbus began to think. Islands such as the Madeiras, the Azores, and the Canaries lay far out in the Atlantic. These places had been discovered by Portuguese ships. Maybe there were other islands even farther out in the ocean.

And there was another curious fact. Every so often, strange objects would float ashore. On the beaches of the Madeiras were found tree trunks, branches, bushes, and roots of plants. But they did not look like the type of trees that grew in Europe.

Once, two dead bodies washed in with the tide. Their faces did not look European. It was thought they might be Chinese. This made Columbus wonder if China might not be very close by.

In truth, the bodies were those of Native Americans. And the Caribbean driftwood had been pushed thousands of miles by the Gulf Stream.

Of course, Columbus was not the only one to marvel about the strange objects. Others also felt very curious. But unlike them, Columbus was determined to investigate. He was not afraid to sail into the Atlantic. He was sure something must be out there.

Not everyone shared his enthusiasm. "The ocean is too rough," one Portuguese captain reported. "Such great distances! Whoever sails too far into the Atlantic will never return."

The more Columbus thought about it, the more confident he became. Before long, he was saying that he could cross the Atlantic and return to Europe safely. Of course, the problem was to convince other people that the idea was practical.

Today there is a myth about Columbus. According to the story, people in his day insisted the earth was flat. Then Columbus came along and proved they were wrong. The truth is that people did realize the earth was shaped like a sphere. From ancient times, learned men in Egypt and Greece agreed this was so. And two hundred years before Columbus, the Italian poet Dante also described a round world.

From experience, sailors were quick to notice the globe was round. Edging down the African coast, Portuguese sea captains soon discovered they were traveling on a curve. In the night sky, stars suddenly vanished behind them. And new stars rose over the bows of the ships. This could only happen if the earth were curved. So Columbus did not worry about falling off the edge of the earth.

Even so, Columbus found very few people who believed in him. Why? It was not the *shape* of the earth. It was the *size* of the earth. His opponents thought the world was much bigger than he did.

Columbus began to study. In the geography books he read, there were figures that guessed the distance between Europe and Asia. To show that the voyage would be short, Columbus copied down the smallest numbers. In that way, he decided that the

distance from the Canary Islands to China was only 3,550 miles. He was completely wrong. The real distance is 11,766 miles.

People more learned than Columbus told him of his mistake. "You'll never sail all the way to the Far East," one person warned. "The earth is much bigger than you think."

Columbus paid no attention. He was already busy planning his expedition to the East Indies. It

would be very, very costly. In addition to ships, he needed sailors, food, and clothing. Paying for all this himself was out of the question. The only person who could pay for such a trip was a monarch.

At the royal palace in Lisbon, King John II met with Columbus. The king of Portugal sat at a table heaped with maps and geography books. He knew a great deal about navigation. He had backed many voyages of exploration. His advisers gathered around.

"Your Majesty," said Columbus, "the distance to the Indies is not great."

The king looked doubtful. He glanced up at his advisers. The experts were shaking their heads.

"He has miscalculated the distance," said one.

"Impossible," said another.

Still, King John did not turn Columbus away. There was something about his confidence that the king liked. He promised to give whatever help he could.

"Well," John finally said, "I'll appoint a special commission to look into the matter."

The king's special commission said no. Still hopeful, John decided to test Columbus's idea. He ordered several ships to sail out into the Atlantic and find the East Indies. Before long, the captains came back to port. They lost their nerve.

In the meantime, much was happening to Columbus. His wife Filipa died in 1485. His son Diego was still a small boy. After Filipa's death, Columbus decided to travel with Diego. From Lisbon, they took a ship to Palos, which was a busy seaport in Spain. After stepping off the ship, they did not remain in the noisy city. Instead, they began to walk. Columbus knew of a Franciscan monastery outside of the town.

The sun blazed hotly. The road was dusty.

"Are you tired, son?" Columbus asked.

"Yes, father," the boy admitted. He was hungry and thirsty, too.

They continued to tramp along. Eventually the walls of the monastery came into sight. Both father and son felt certain they could count on the kind Franciscans.

Columbus was very religious. He had been named for Saint Christopher, the patron saint of travelers. Under the saint's protection, he prayed he would always have a safe journey.

Diego and Columbus finally reached the monastery. At the gate of the monastery Columbus rang the bell. They waited. Soon a porter came out. He asked who they were.

"I'm Christopher Columbus of Genoa," answered Columbus. "I ask your hospitality for my son and myself."

The porter nodded. "We never turn travelers away," he said. "Follow me. We will share whatever we have with you."

The Franciscans lived a simple life. The monks worked in the fields. They told Columbus how much they enjoyed their work. At their prayers, they felt great peace of mind. Palos was nearby. But they felt no desire to visit the city.

Soon the head of the monastery came to greet the visitors. Columbus explained the reason for his visit to Spain. He intended to see the king and queen.

"That might be difficult, Master Columbus," said the monk. "Have you not heard? We're fighting a war against the Moors."

Columbus knew that the Moors had invaded many centuries earlier. Crossing from North Africa through the Strait of Gibraltar, people who believed in the faith of Islam conquered most of Spain. The Catholics called them infidels. The Moors were powerful fighters. They would not be easy to defeat.

The monk went on, "The king and queen think of nothing but the war."

Columbus supposed he was right. It meant that getting a royal meeting would take time.

The monks invited Columbus and Diego to share their meal.

"We have only simple food," one monk said. "But you are welcome to it."

Everyone sat at a rough wooden table. They ate bread and cheese. The delicious vegetables had been grown in the monastery garden.

Columbus and Diego finished their meal. But Columbus had been thinking. He said to the monks, "While I am waiting, I'd like to leave Diego here. I know he would be in good hands. Would that be possible?"

"Of course," said the monk. "He may stay as long as you wish."

One of the Franciscans was curious. He said to Columbus, "What is your business in Spain?"

Columbus was almost afraid to answer. He had been laughed at so often. Finally he said, "I hope to receive royal help for a voyage."

The Franciscan stroked his beard. "But many Spaniards have sailed to Africa. That should be easy to arrange."

Columbus smiled at him. "Not to Africa. I'm going across the Atlantic to the Indies."

The next morning Columbus set off for the palace. As he had feared, the king and queen were busy. So he settled down to wait.

During the following months, he met a woman named Beatriz Enriquez de Harana. His wife was dead and he was lonely. There was nothing to prevent his marrying Beatriz if he wished. They had a son. His name was Ferdinand. Years later, Ferdinand Columbus would write about his father's voyages to the New World.

After a year or so, Columbus learned that the king and queen would see him at last. He hurried to the city of Cordova. But the meeting turned out to be disappointing. King Ferdinand showed absolutely no interest. Only the queen listened. She asked many questions. Columbus's confidence impressed her. In the end, she agreed to consider his idea. Her advisers would study the plan.

"But even if they approve," she warned Columbus, "I still can't help you now. Your voyage is very costly." Only when the last Moorish fortress in Spain had fallen would she have time for exploration.

"But the royal army stands on the brink of victory," Columbus said.

The queen shrugged. "The war will end when we take the city of Granada. Who knows when that will be?"

Isabella promised she would keep Columbus in mind. With that he had to be satisfied.

Before long, news of Columbus's meeting with Isabella drifted back to Portugal. King John heard about it. He began to feel worried. The last thing he wanted was to lose Columbus to the Spaniards. So he asked Columbus to come back to Lisbon.

Now Columbus faced a serious choice. Which was better? A vague promise from the Spanish queen or fairly strong interest from the king of Portugal? He decided his chances might be better with the Portuguese.

With high hopes, Columbus hurried to Lisbon. But he found the king still unready to give a definite answer. Once again, he was obliged to bide his time.

For the next two years Columbus continued to wait. Then, in 1488, he suffered a terrible blow. A Portuguese explorer named Bartholomew Dias sailed down the west coast of Africa. At the southern tip of Africa, he rounded the Cape of Good Hope. Then he sailed up the coast of east Africa.

This successful voyage proved that India and all of Asia could be reached by sailing around Africa. Ten years later, Vasco da Gama would follow the Dias route. He would sail around Africa, cross the Arabian Sea, and land on the coast of India.

After Bartholomew Dias reached the Cape, King John lost all interest in Columbus. Crossing the Atlantic would be an incredible expense. Why should the king waste his money? Now there was an easy route to the East Indies.

Columbus was informed of the king's decision. The answer was no. And this time it was final.

His brother Bartholomew had come to Lisbon for a visit. Bartholomew did his best to console him. But it was terribly discouraging. Columbus was thirty-seven years old. How could he give up his life's dream?

"What will you do now?" asked Bartholomew.

"Try somewhere else," Christopher replied.

Other European nations also were interested in exploration. For instance, the kings of England or France might like the idea.

But then Columbus wondered if he should go back to the Spanish court again. Queen Isabella's advisers were still considering the idea. It was true that the queen had given him little encouragement. And the war against the Moors was not over. Certainly the Spanish had not yet captured the city of Granada.

However, Columbus admired King Ferdinand and Queen Isabella. On that basis, he made his decision. He would return to Spain. First, he would visit his son, Diego. Then he would ask to see the king and queen of Spain once more.

The Great Enterprise

I n 1489, Columbus journeyed back to Spain. First he went to visit the monastery near Palos. He was eager to see Diego. Then he sought another meeting with Queen Isabella.

The queen received him with courtesy. As always, her manner was gracious. But she could give him no hope. The war with the Moors still continued. It occupied the thoughts of both herself and Ferdinand. Besides, Isabella's advisers thought Columbus was wrong. They insisted that the earth was much larger than Columbus claimed. Unknown to Columbus, they were right.

"Pray be patient, Master Columbus," the queen urged. "How can I make a decision now? My royal commission has not finished its report."

By this time Columbus had a lot of experience with royal commissions. But he bowed his head. "I will be patient," he said. "Your Majesty gives me hope."

England and France could wait. For the time being, he decided to stay in Spain and hear Isabella's decision. During these months he was busy studying his books and maps. Many a long day he spent checking numbers. By the light of flickering candles, he would read until late at night. Sometimes he fell asleep at his table just as dawn was breaking.

Many people had told him that he was mistaken about the size of the earth. But he ignored their warnings. He couldn't believe his figures were wrong. And the more he studied the more convinced he became.

His problem was this: He was making the circumference of the globe too short by one quarter. No wonder he thought it possible to make a quick trip to the East Indies.

He went on talking to anyone who would listen. Merchants who sent their cargo ships on the high seas were intrigued. They favored exploring the Atlantic beyond the Canary Islands.

Some geographers also approved. One man said, "Who can say if you're right or wrong? But all those islands—the Madeiras, the Canaries, Cape Verde—they were once unknown. Why shouldn't you seek more unknown islands beyond them?"

This annoyed Columbus. "Because I'm not hunting for unknown islands," he snapped. "I'm looking for a new route to the East Indies! And I intend to find it, too."

This was always his attitude, whether he was speaking to a king or to a sailor. Clinging to his vision was a struggle sometimes. But he wanted support for a full-fledged expedition across the Atlantic. He would not settle for anything less.

In some respects, his future depended on the war against the Moors. Thus, he followed the war news carefully. The armies of Ferdinand and Isabella were steadily pushing south. One Moorish city after another fell.

Columbus prayed for a speedy victory. Not only did he have a personal reason. But he also was a Catholic. As a Christian, he hoped to see the Catholics defeat the Moslems.

In 1490, Columbus finally heard from the king and queen. Called to the court, he hurried to obey. After a warm greeting, the king asked Isabella to explain the reason they wished to see Columbus.

"The royal commission has submitted its report," she announced. "I am sorry to say that their report is unfavorable."

Columbus could not hide his disappointment. His shoulders sagged. After a moment, he spoke quietly. "Then Your Majesty will not support my expedition?"

To his surprise, the queen shook her head. "The king and I haven't made up our minds," she replied. "The report is not the last word."

Confused, he listened as the queen went on speaking. Perhaps they would give their approval after all. Who knew? But first Spain had to be freed from the Moors.

So nothing had changed.

Before leaving, Columbus politely asked Queen Isabella why the royal commission had ruled against his idea.

The queen said, "They believe the voyage would take three years."

"Three years!" exclaimed Columbus. "They're wrong. I can go there and return in only one year."

This made the queen pause. Perhaps Columbus was right. What a wonderful triumph it would be for Spain!

"We will meet again," she told him. "At another time."

The royal audience was over.

Walking back to his lodgings, Columbus wondered how long he would have to wait this time.

Onward to the East From the West

The months rolled by. No word came from the king and queen of Spain. It looked as if the war might drag on for a long while. Columbus made up his mind to leave Spain. It was time to try his luck with the French.

In 1491, Columbus visited the Franciscan monastery near Palos. He had missed Diego. He decided to take his son with him to France. At the monastery, he spoke to Father Juan Perez. He explained the reason for his journey to France.

"I'm tired of waiting," Columbus complained to the head of the Franciscans. "Perhaps my luck will change for the better with the king of France."

Perez thought it was a terrible idea. "You must not go," he told Columbus. "I believe in your voyage. You must sail for Spain!"

Columbus shrugged. "What can I do?" he said. "I've been here for years. And still I haven't won the favor of the king and queen."

By this time, Columbus doubted if he would ever receive a favorable answer. Certainly this would not happen so long as the war continued.

Father Perez looked thoughtful. Finally he said, "Let me see if I can help. Once I was the

queen's confessor. I'll go to court and see Her Majesty."

"But what can you possibly say to her?" Columbus wondered.

"That she will lose a great opportunity if you leave Spain," Father Perez said. He made Columbus promise to stay at the monastery until his return.

Father Perez's visit to court proved successful. He persuaded Queen Isabella to speak with Columbus. And so once again he found himself bowing to the powerful queen. Much to his relief, some of the royal advisers had changed their minds. Now they spoke in favor of the voyage.

However, new objections arose. This time it was not Columbus's *plan*. Instead, the queen was displeased about other things. For example, Columbus had asked for the title of admiral. Another title he demanded was viceroy of the king. And that was not all. He expected to discover new lands. And he expected one tenth of the income from the new lands to be his. For his son Diego he wanted a position at court as a page. And after his death, Columbus wanted his son to inherit his titles. That seemed only fair to Columbus.

The queen could not believe her ears. "Master Columbus," she said, "you ask a high price."

"Only what I'm worth," he said with pride.

Turning away, the queen said she would think over his demands.

Columbus had never dreamed that the delay would go on so long. Then in January 1492, Granada was captured by the Spanish army. At last the war with the Moors was over. It was the great moment that Columbus had been looking forward to. Now there was nothing to distract Ferdinand and Isabella. Surely they would agree to finance his trip.

But to his shock, something unbelievable happened. He learned that his proposal was being turned down. This time it was final. Columbus must have felt cruelly used. He had been refused first by Portugal, now Spain. But that still left the French. He began making plans to visit France.

As soon as possible he left the Spanish court. However, he had traveled only a short distance when he was stopped. A messenger on horseback came pounding up behind him. He said that Columbus must turn around and return. It was an order from the queen.

Columbus arrived at court. Queen Isabella was smiling. She had changed her mind. He could have the titles of admiral and viceroy. Indeed, she agreed to all of his demands. Whatever he wished for would be his. Somehow she would find the money. If necessary, she would pawn her jewels to pay for the expedition. Overjoyed, Columbus knelt before the queen.

The years of waiting were over. The disappointments lay behind him. Now he had the

royal backing he needed. The great idea could become
real at last.

Never had Columbus been tempted to give up.
Never had he abandoned his dream. He had learned
the importance of persistence.

Royal approval was the first step. Now
Columbus had to lead the expedition across the
Atlantic. At once he began to prepare a sailing fleet.

It was decided that three ships should make the voyage. Their names were the *Santa Maria,* the *Pinta,* and the *Nina.*

Outfitting the fleet required a great deal of care. But Columbus was an experienced captain. He knew that he faced a long ocean voyage. It was important to select the right crew for the ships. What kind of seamen would be best? Of course, they would have to be exceptionally fearless. Storms and hurricanes could not bother them.

But there was something even more important. Not being able to see land terrified many sailors. For Columbus's crew, there would be nothing but water for weeks at a time. The days would be long and boring. Only strong men could endure such conditions.

Finding sailors was not easy. Many sailors refused to go with Columbus. They thought the trip meant sure death. There was no choice but to use some prisoners. A few of these were murderers who had been sentenced to death. If they returned alive, they would get their freedom. But Columbus was a good judge of people. Almost all the prisoners turned out to be excellent sailors.

To command the *Nina* and the *Pinta*, Columbus hired a pair of brothers. Their names were Martin Alonza Pinzon and Vincente Yanez Pinzon. The largest of three ships, the *Santa Maria*, would be commanded by Columbus himself.

The *Santa Maria* is the most famous ship in history. But few facts are known about her. Like all of Columbus's ships, she had three masts. There was a large mainsail. It was set slightly forward where it could catch the wind.

Another person who went on the voyage was a man who knew several languages. Columbus needed someone who would be able to speak to the natives in the East Indies. So he chose Luis de Torres, who could speak Hebrew and Arabic. He thought these languages would be known there.

The day of departure was set for August 3, 1492. At Palos, everyone attended church. Then the crew climbed aboard. The sails were unfurled. The fleet swept out of the harbor. Before long, the green shore had disappeared. Sea birds circled overhead.

Six days later, they reached the Canary Islands. One of the ships was having trouble. Martin Alonza Pinzon raised a flag that asked for help. The *Pinta's* rudder had worked loose. Steering her was becoming difficult. Columbus boarded the *Pinta* to look. There was no choice but to stop for repairs.

When the *Pinta* was seaworthy again, they sailed on. Now the Canary Islands were behind Columbus. Ahead of him lay open water. He glided into the unknown.

Day after day, the waves rolled on. August went by. The sun burned butter-yellow. September came. All around, the sea stretched to the horizon.

On September 16, the pilot of the *Santa Maria* suddenly called to Columbus. "Look, admiral," cried Juan de La Cosa, "there are weeds in the water." He was pointing over the side of the ship.

Columbus looked and saw a strange sight. A great carpet of green and brown slime was floating on the surface of the water. These weeds were algae, which are known today as sargasso.

The weeds made La Cosa nervous. "Can we sail through this?" he asked. "What if we get stuck? We'll be stranded here forever!"

But the weeds did not alarm Columbus. They were not thick enough to stop the ships. "Don't worry," he said calmly. "Keep the *Santa Maria* on course. We'll lead the way."

The *Santa Maria* cut a path through the Sargasso Sea. The *Pinta* and *Nina* trailed behind. Eventually, the frightened sailors got used to the weeds. Columbus had insisted they could navigate through the sea of slime. Now they realized he was right. Their confidence in him increased.

Some of the sailors thought that the weeds came from an island. They wanted to hunt for it.

Columbus shook his head. "We're not seeking any islands. The East Indies is our destination. Nothing must delay us."

It was fortunate that the ships did not stop and search. None of them knew it, but sargasso floats freely on the water. No island was anywhere near. They were in the middle of the Atlantic Ocean.

For a while the expedition made good progress. They ran into the North Atlantic trade winds. The sails billowed out. The ships rushed along. All the men felt pleased.

But then came a day when the trade winds were left behind. The sails collapsed. The ships began to drift. They were hardly moving at all.

One thing that sailors dread is complete calm. That happens when the wind is too weak to move a ship forward. Columbus's crew began to worry.

"Be patient," Columbus urged. "Our course will take us back into the trade winds. Besides, we're not far from the Indies." All they had to do, he said, was to keep on going. He offered a prize for the first man who sighted land.

After that everyone strained their eyes. Peering into the distance, each sailor hoped he would win the prize. Equally important, everyone was eager to reach land and step ashore.

Eventually, the wind picked up. The ships gained speed. Relieved, the men told each other that the admiral was right after all.

Meanwhile, the crew had noticed unusual birds flying overhead. Some of the birds fluttered down. They even perched on the masts of the ships.

"A land bird!" shouted one of the sailors. "We're near land!" There was cheering on all three ships.

At once Columbus ordered a test. A lead weight was dropped over the side of the ship by a rope. He waited to see if the weight would hit the bottom of the ocean. If so, it meant they were in shallow water. And land could not be far away. But the lead weight did not touch bottom. It is no wonder, because the Atlantic is more than 10,000 feet deep at that point!

Again the ships slowed down. Now the winds began blowing from the wrong direction. The wind was against them. The men began to complain. Columbus said, "Look at it this way. On our return voyage, these very same winds will be with us. They'll fill our sails and carry us home."

When the men heard this, they smiled. "Hurrah for the admiral," they began calling out.

Columbus was a good judge of human beings. He realized that the men wondered if they would ever see Spain again. Removing their fears was important. They needed encouragement. Again and again he would offer just the right words to inspire them. One of his slogans was "Onward to the East from the West!"

At dusk on September 25, a great shout rose from the *Pinta*. It was Martin Alonzo Pinzon. His cries could be heard on board the other ships.

He was pointing toward the horizon. "Land, land!" he yelled. "I claim the reward! I was the first to see land!"

Sailors began climbing into the rigging. Soon they were all shouting—all but Columbus. He stayed calm. But he did order a change of course. They began heading in the direction to which Pinzon had pointed. Night was beginning to fall. Soon it was dark.

Columbus ordered the ships to slow down. He warned his pilot to watch out for reefs. It would be a tragedy to run aground in the darkness. With great caution, they moved forward. Frequently, the lead weight was lowered into the deep, dark water.

Finally, the sun rose. There was no land in sight. But still hoping, the men continued to scan the horizon. Columbus kept going until late afternoon. Then he ordered his pilot to take the *Santa Maria* back to its old course.

"Pinzon was wrong," he said. "He saw a patch of sky. Or maybe it was a cloud on the horizon. But it wasn't land."

Disappointed, the sailors returned to their duties. In fact, Columbus never believed it was land. According to his calculations, they were nowhere near the Indies. He only investigated because his figures just might be wrong. When they failed to find Pinzon's "land," it proved that Columbus was on the right course. After this, he took care to stick with his original plan—sail West to reach the East.

The men on the ships, however, were not so confident of Columbus's vision. Sometimes they trusted him. Whenever he seemed to be right, they were willing to follow his orders. But at other times, they worried. They had seen that he also could be wrong.

"He went looking for land the other day," a sailor said. "Then he said it was a cloud."

"That's right," another man agreed. "He got fooled, too."

Some of the sailors wondered if Columbus was fooling himself. Was it possible that he had no idea about the location of the East Indies? If so, he was making fools of everyone.

Unknown to them, they were half right. Columbus *was* tricking them. Since leaving Palos, he had been keeping two logs. In one book, he recorded phony figures. But he also had a secret log. In this one, he wrote down the real distance they had traveled. If the men knew how far they had come from Spain they would be terrified.

Even so, the crew was in a sour mood. One day was like the next. There was nothing to do but keep the ship clean and stare at the water. The blue of the sky and sea filled their eyes.

As the days went on, fear mounted. The men whispered among themselves. Some warned that the ships had already journeyed too far into the unknown. They were doomed.

Others expressed a bit of hope. Probably they were nearing the point of no return. There was still time to turn back. Later, it would be impossible. But they must act before it was too late.

Columbus ignored the grumbling. But one day, the crew of the *Santa Maria* stopped working. They told the admiral they thought it was time to go home.

"Turn around?" Columbus exclaimed. He threw up his arms. "Never will you hear me give such an order."

He struggled to remain calm. It was clear that the men were close to mutiny. Some of them threatened to take command of the ship.

Columbus answered coldly. "When we get back to Spain, I will testify against you. Queen Isabella will have you hanged."

"We can throw you overboard," somebody snarled.

"You'll still be hanged," Columbus warned his crew.

There was silence. The men began to look uncertain. Thinking quickly, Columbus began speaking.

"Think of the East Indies," Columbus said. "Think of all the gold. When we get home—and we *will* get home—you'll be rich. Every man here will be a hero. In your villages, people will forever salute you. Your neighbors will say you sailed on the most daring voyage in history."

By the time he had finished, the men were cheering him. Minutes later, they were back at work. Some were watching over the bow of the ship for land. Columbus's pep talk had soothed them. It had also rekindled their enthusiasm. Most important, order was restored again.

Under a clear blue sky, the vessels plowed through the water. The sailors could see enormous fish darting about in the waves. Sometimes a dolphin broke the surface. Then it fell back with a mighty splash. By now, more birds screamed in the sky. Some of them did not seem to be sea gulls. They looked like land birds. Encouraged, the seamen hoped that land would appear soon.

The weeks passed. Now it was October. There had been good weather. Fresh wind filled the sails. Steadily, the three ships plunged forward. The sailors had begun spending all of their free time on deck. All they could talk about was spotting land. At any moment trees might suddenly appear.

"That prize is going to be mine," one man boasted. "Because I intend to be first."

A burst of laughter was heard.

"We all want the prize," another sailor told him. "Any of us might get it."

Every morning now, they stared at the driftwood floating on the water. There was a lot of it. Unlike the seaweed seen earlier, this was not wet or slimy. These trees and bushes did not come from the cold, deep sea. They had grown in the earth.

All doubt about whether they would ever reach land again was gone. The *Santa Maria,* the *Pinta,* and the *Nina* were really nearing land.

At night the ships slowed down. Always cautious, Columbus was being extra careful. If a ship hit an unseen rock, it might sink. Then its crew would never reach Spain again. The pilots could not see very far ahead. In the pitch black, they struggled to avoid some last minute disaster.

The New World Is Discovered

At dawn on October 11, signs of land began to appear. On all three ships, men saw branches floating in the water. There were green leaves on the branches. A piece of bamboo was hauled aboard the *Pinta*. A sailor on the *Nina* even discovered a berry bush. Not too long ago it had been growing in the earth. Some of its berries were still attached to the branches.

However, they saw no land. Water continued to surround them. And it was true that debris could

float a long, long way. Columbus remembered how driftwood had traveled on the Gulf Stream to the Canary Islands. Still, he felt hopeful. They were sure to strike land if they just kept on their course.

"I want every man on the alert," he ordered.

There were no maps to guide them. Finding their own way in these unknown waters was tricky. But Columbus wasn't going to let anything happen now. After all, they were near the East Indies.

Of course, Columbus and his ships were really thousands of miles from the *East* Indies. But they were getting close to the *West* Indies.

There was no need for Columbus to remind the crew about his promise. Nobody had forgotten the reward for sighting land.

That day the seamen noticed flowers. Rising and falling on the waves were lovely blossoms. Never before had the men seen flowers like these. Yet, still no land appeared.

Darkness fell. Cautiously, the three ships edged forward. The pilots feared shallow water that might be filled with rocks.

Everyone had trouble sleeping. But Columbus did not even think of sleep. He stood in the bow of the *Santa Maria* and looked out at the black night. He strained to see. Where was the land?

Suddenly he spotted something. It looked like a light. He called to a sailor standing nearby. Pointing, he asked Pedro Gutierrez if he saw anything.

"Yes, sir!" cried Gutierrez. "It's a light that comes and goes. Maybe it's land."

Another sailor ran over. But he saw no light. It was a false alarm.

The vigil went on. The men kept constant watch. The ships were taking care to stay close together. They did not wish to lose contact with each other.

Midnight passed. It was now the dark morning of October 12. The sea was calm and silent. Then, a little after 2:00 a.m., a shriek was heard aboard the *Pinta*. The sound echoed across the silvery water. It was the voice of Rodrigo de Triana, the lookout.

"Land!" he shouted. "Land! Land!"

Martin Alonzo Pinzon came running. "Where?" he demanded.

"Up ahead, sir. It's a light."

Triana was right. Now, everybody on the *Pinta* could see the light. It was gleaming on the shore.

The sailors went wild with excitement. Over and over, they yelled, "Land! Land! We made it!"

At once, Pinzon ordered the *Pinta's* cannon to be fired. This was a signal to the *Santa Maria* and the *Nina*. It meant that land had definitely been sighted.

Columbus heard the boom. He ordered his pilot to bring the ship close to the *Pinta*.

"Pinzon," he called. "Are you sure?"

"Absolutely," Pinzon answered. "Look over there, admiral. You'll see it, too."

Now Columbus could see the light. There was no doubt about it. He felt certain they had reached the East Indies.

The *Pinta* drew alongside her sister ships. Nobody was sleeping now. The news brought cheering and yelling. Finally, Columbus ordered them to quiet down.

"Stay alert," he warned. "Look out for rocks. And look out for ships. We mustn't ram any East Indian ships."

That was one danger they needn't have worried about. The Native Americans did not build large ships. They used canoes. Their tiny boats would offer no threat to the European ships.

Dawn began to break. The sky lightened. The shore of an island slowly moved into view. Columbus and his crew saw a beach. The surf rolled up over the sand, stopped, and then rolled back. Beyond the beach stood tall trees. All around grew lush green plants and bushes.

"There must be people here," said Juan de La Cosa, the pilot of the *Santa Maria*.

"Undoubtedly, La Cosa," agreed Columbus. "Where there's fire, there are people."

But no people could be seen on the beach. Columbus decided they must live elsewhere on the island. Perhaps their homes were built deeper in the woods.

He wondered if the people would be friendly. There was no reason why they should be unfriendly. Didn't Marco Polo travel all over the Far East? As far as Columbus recalled, Marco Polo received a warm welcome wherever he went. Columbus expected that he would get the same kind of treatment.

That morning, there was much to do. Columbus began to give orders. They must look for a good place to drop anchor. So Martin Alonzo Pinzon began guiding the *Pinta* along the shore. Whenever he came to a rocky area, he edged away quickly. Soundings were made constantly with a weighted lead. Pinzon had to make sure the water was deep enough, but not too deep. If the anchor did not reach the bottom, the ship would float away.

Finally, the *Pinta* came to a place where the shore curved inward. In this cove, the water was peaceful. The depth of the water seemed just right. The anchor was scraping the bottom. Here the ships could come to a safe rest.

As a signal, Pinzon fired his cannon. Then the *Santa Maria* and the *Nina* hurried to join the *Pinta*.

In the cove, the three ships anchored together. Columbus held a meeting with the Pinzon brothers. It was decided the fleet should remain in the cove for now. The next step was to go ashore and explore the island they had discovered.

At anchor at last, the sailors were eager to rush ashore. But the admiral reminded them of their duties. They were to stay and look after the ships.

Soon three small boats were lowered into the water. Columbus, the Pinzon brothers, and a number of sailors rowed to shore.

This day—October 12, 1492—would become one of the most memorable dates in human history. It is the date when the New World was discovered. Hundreds of years later, it is still celebrated as Columbus Day. In both North and South America, nations continue to honor Columbus.

Columbus was the first European to actually place his feet in the New World. It was only fair that the honor should be his. Carrying a flag, he knelt in the sand. Behind him stood his captains. Columbus began to speak. His words rang out strong and clear in the bright air.

"In the name of Queen Isabella and King Ferdinand of Spain," he said, "I take possession of this land."

Then he made a small hole in the sand with the tip of his sword. Firmly, he planted the flag of the *Santa Maria*.

Columbus knew it was important that his words be written down. A notary was asked to come forward with his pen. Then Columbus continued.

"I will name this island San Salvador." He turned to the notary. "Are you taking this down? You have heard me state this before two witnesses." He gestured to Martin Alonzo and Vincente Pinzon.

Still kneeling, Columbus asked his captains to make the following promise: "I vow to obey the viceroy of these newly discovered lands, the admiral of the Great Ocean, the governor of the Indies."

The Pinzon brothers solemnly agreed.

At that moment, there was a rustling of leaves. Out of the forest crept a band of people. They came forward cautiously. It was clear they felt frightened. But they also were very curious. Who were these strange-looking creatures with their huge ships?

Slowly the people drew closer. Suddenly they realized that the Spaniards were human beings like themselves. At this point, they rushed up to meet these strangers from the sea.

Columbus was eager to speak to the natives. It was for this reason that he had brought along the man who knew Hebrew and Arabic. Columbus waited while Luis de Torres talked in Arabic. There was no reply from the island people.

Then Torres tried Hebrew. Once again, the natives looked puzzled. It was clear they hadn't the slightest idea of what he was saying. Finally, Torres had to give up. Obviously, the islanders did not understand either Hebrew or Arabic.

Columbus was frustrated. He had been sure that at least one of the two languages would be known in the East Indies. All his careful preparations had been for nothing. There seemed to be no way to talk with these people.

Even so, the natives were the most fascinating humans Columbus had ever seen. He could not help staring at them. They wore practically no clothing. The color of their skins was reddish brown. They had short, straight hair.

Most surprising was their behavior. They were gentle as lambs. Meek and mild, the natives carried no weapons. They seemed to be quite trusting.

Another thing also was clear to Columbus. The natives did not seem to know anything about the

Spanish. They thought that Columbus and his sailors had risen magically out of the sea.

Not understanding one another caused confusion. Columbus did not know what to call the red people. So he named them "Indians." He still believed he had reached the Indies.

To show his good will, Columbus decided to give the Indians a few presents. With him from Spain he had brought a supply of trinkets. Mostly these trinkets were rings and other decorations of no real value. But the Indians had never seen anything like them. So they thought the cheap gifts were most unusual and marvelous.

The day passed quickly. From the ships came carpenters and woodworkers. They built a huge wooden cross. Then Columbus had the new crucifix set on a small hill where everyone could see it. It was to be a symbol of thanksgiving.

Columbus had called the island San Salvador. But the Native Americans had their own name for their home. To them, the island was Guanahani.

Today the tiny speck of land has an even different name. On a map of the Bahamas, it is Watling Island.

Five hundred years later, Watling Island is mainly known for its lovely beaches. But the island will always have a special place in history. It is the spot where Columbus happened to land when he discovered America.

The New World

olumbus spent two days at San Salvador. Before long, the Indians had become much bolder. They wanted to be friendly. The Indians were Arawaks. Long ago, their ancestors had migrated from South America. By no means could they be called savages. They knew how to spin cloth and make pottery. And they built sturdy huts for their homes.

By nature, the Arawaks were not warlike. Sometimes they were obliged to defend themselves against a brutal people called the Caribs. In war, they armed themselves with short spears. But whenever possible, they preferred to live in peace.

The Spaniards were amazed to see the Indians wearing rings and necklaces made of real gold. The natives took these ornaments for granted. They were perfectly happy to trade precious rings for worthless trinkets. Where did all their gold come from? The Europeans were impatient to find out.

The greed of his men worried Columbus. The Indians were innocent and helpless. The Spanish could take whatever they wanted. But Columbus hesitated. He did not wish to anger the Indians. Besides, he wanted to convert them to the Catholic faith. How was he to gain riches for Spain, for his men—and for himself?

The "Indies"

olumbus began to explore nearby islands. On these visits he met many men and women. He still called them "Indians." By now, he was using sign language to talk.

To honor the queen of Spain, Columbus named one of the islands Isabella. This island was especially beautiful. Its climate was sweet and mild. There were birds and animals he had never seen before. Everywhere bloomed lush flowers and trees. Some of the plants were good for healing sickness.

Columbus was enchanted. "I could never tire of looking at all these amazing things," he declared.

The friendly natives living on Isabella made him feel at home. The chief invited him to explore the island. Columbus could not help staring at the chief's robe. It was decorated with gold.

Eventually, Columbus reached Cuba. This is the largest island in the Caribbean. Cuba was so big that its size confused Columbus. He decided it might be part of the mainland. This was an exciting idea. He believed the mainland must be China or even Japan.

He sent out a search party to find the capital city of the Great Khan. Columbus wished to pay respect to the emperor. As was the custom, he sent greetings from the king of Spain.

Much to his disappointment, the search party would return with bad news. It found no emperor, only Indians.

Meanwhile, something happened to upset Columbus. The *Pinta* vanished. Martin Alonzo Pinzon had been growing impatient. He was not satisfied with Columbus and his leadership. In his opinion, the admiral was going about things in the wrong way. An Indian told Pinzon about an island rich in gold. So Pinzon took the *Pinta* and sailed away to find it.

Columbus had no trouble guessing the reason for Pinzon's flight. The lure was gold. There was no way of knowing if he would ever see the *Pinta* again.

By this time he was busy exploring Cuba. Its size had surprised him. Now he kept discovering more and more unusual facts. For example, he learned that the island did not have a ruler. Neither Europeans nor Christians had visited there before.

Columbus decided this information would be of great interest to King Ferdinand. He described the island. A notary wrote down his words. "The land is ripe for conversion to our glorious Christian religion," he remarked.

It is true that Columbus was excited by new lands and by wealth. But his voyage also had a religious purpose. Sailing with him were several missionaries. These men of the Catholic Church told the natives about their religion.

By now, conversation with the Indians was becoming easier. The Spaniards were beginning to learn the languages of the islands. But some sign language was still required.

Wherever he went, Columbus called the Indians together. A crowd would gather in a village or on the beach. Then the missionaries would begin to preach. The natives seemed to like the new religion. More and more of them made up their minds to follow the Catholic beliefs.

This made Columbus feel extremely proud. In those days, it was considered important to bring religion to those who were not Christians. Columbus felt as if he were working for God.

Leaving Cuba, he went on to another large island. He called it Hispaniola. Today, this island is shared by two countries—Haiti and the Dominican Republic. Columbus stayed on board the *Santa Maria*. He sent a group of men ashore to explore. Their instructions were to travel inland and meet the people. But more important, the men were to keep their eyes open. Did the Indians have gold? If so, where did they get it?

"Try to find out if there are any gold mines," he said. "Draw maps so we can locate the mines."

The search party discovered several villages. To their delight, they met Indians wearing gold on their clothing. But they had no success in finding gold mines. All they discovered were a few nuggets of gold in the streams. This was disappointing. They sought great quantities of the precious metal. The men had to return empty-handed to the *Santa Maria*.

Columbus did not understand something. The gold worn by the Indians did not come from the Caribbean islands. The gold was mined in Mexico and Central America. Indians on the mainland traded gold ornaments to people on nearby islands. Then, these people traded with islands farther out in the Caribbean.

During this period of history, explorers believed it was possible to find incredible wealth. In new lands, the cities would be built of gold. They expected to see people living in golden castles and eating from golden plates.

Eventually, the Spanish did discover large amounts of gold. About 25 years later, Ferdinand Cortez and his men landed in Mexico. They conquered a wealthy people called the Aztecs.

But Columbus failed to find great riches. The search party returned from Hispaniola. In some ways, their report was favorable. The island contained plenty of good food and water. Streams were filled with fish. Banana trees grew everywhere. Best of all, the people were peaceful.

Columbus decided to found a settlement at Hispaniola. His men began to build thatched huts like those the Indians lived in. Some of the natives also helped in this work. Around the group of huts was erected a wall. This stockade was made mostly of tall, heavy tree trunks. It was clear that people on Hispaniola were peaceful. But Columbus worried that unfriendly Indians might arrive and attack his settlement. So he wanted protection.

The settlement was named La Navidad. It was the first European dwelling place in the New World.

Then Columbus told his crew that some of them would remain at La Navidad. "On my next voyage, I'll bring more men and I'll take you home."

The sailors looked doubtful. How could they be sure the admiral would really return?

Columbus calmed their fears. The king and queen had made him their viceroy here. In the future, he planned to make many voyages.

"There are more islands to explore," he told them. "And someday I'm going to reach the mainland."

By now, Columbus had many chances to meet the natives. An Indian leader and some of his followers were invited aboard the *Santa Maria*. Columbus offered them food. He observed their gentle manners. When they had gone, he remarked, "How easy it would be to control these people. They'll make good slaves. They won't fight."

Like many others of his day, Columbus believed in slavery. He saw nothing wrong with turning the Native Americans into slaves. In his opinion, the Indians should work for Spanish masters.

Belief in slavery was a great failing of Columbus's. Unfortunately, these ideas were followed by other Spaniards who came after Columbus to the New World. Eventually, these explorers would win over many Indians to the Catholic faith. But they also made them slaves. Men of the church thought this was wrong. But nobody listened to the missionaries.

La Navidad was to be Columbus's permanent colony. But there also was a practical reason for it. While sailing along the coast of Hispaniola, the crew of the *Santa Maria* suffered a terrible accident. On Christmas Eve, 1492, the *Santa Maria* ran aground. It was wrecked.

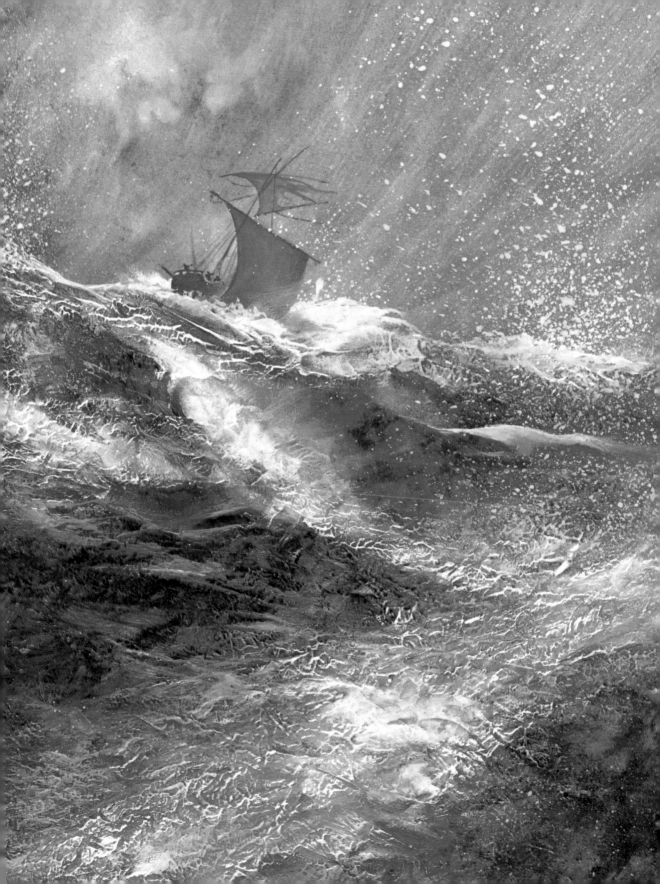

That night, Columbus was asleep in his cabin. The pilot, Juan de La Cosa, was in charge of the ship. But La Cosa also went to sleep. He left the steering to another. Suddenly a dreadful crash was heard. Then the alarm bell sounded. Everyone on board woke up. Columbus rushed to the deck. The ship had skidded to a stop.

"Admiral," said La Cosa, "we're grounded on a reef."

The problem was to float the *Santa Maria* into deeper water. Frantically, the crew struggled to free the ship from the coral reef. But it was wedged too tightly. Huge waves pounded against the ship. Soon the timbers of the *Santa Maria* began to give way. Water started pouring in.

It became clear that the ship was a complete loss. Columbus and his crew were obliged to transfer to the *Nina*. This was a sad ending for Columbus's famous flagship. After the loss of his ship, the admiral held Juan de La Cosa responsible for the disaster. Never again would Columbus trust La Cosa as a pilot of one of his ships.

The loss of the *Santa Maria* was one of the reasons for the building of La Navidad. Now it was impossible to take all the men back. The *Nina* was not big enough for two crews. Sailors from the *Santa Maria* were assigned to stay in Hispaniola. Some of the wood from the ruined flagship was even used in building the stockade at La Navidad.

Meanwhile, the *Pinta* suddenly reappeared. Martin Alonzo Pinzon had failed to find the gold he so wanted. Forgiving him, Columbus invited him to come back and join them. Pinzon accepted.

Three months had passed. It was time to go home. On January 16, 1493, the *Pinta* and the *Nina* headed into the Atlantic. Columbus's new flagship was the *Nina*. Aboard was a group of Indians. Columbus was bringing them back with him. In Spain, he intended to show them off to King Ferdinand and Queen Isabella.

Everyone was eager to get back. Perhaps Columbus was most eager of all.

On the passage home, the sailors sang at their work. There was good reason for their happiness. This time they were not sailing into the unknown. There was no cause for alarm. They were simply crossing an ocean they now knew.

Going to the New World, the crew had come close to rebellion. It was different now. They knew the admiral had guided them safely across the ocean. Now they believed he would get them home again.

Columbus's skill was even more remarkable on this voyage. Out in the Atlantic, the ships ran into heavy storms. In the gale, the winds blew into their faces. The *Nina's* crew had to move the sails back and forth to make any headway. Another time, winds blew the *Nina* off course.

Still, Columbus managed to stick to his route.

The Viceroy

The *Nina* and the *Pinta* were almost home. Suddenly, near the Azores, huge waves and high winds battered the ships. During the storm, they lost sight of one another. To escape the weather, Columbus had no choice but to land in the Azores. The Azores are a group of nine islands in the North Atlantic. There was no sign of the *Pinta*. But he knew that Martin Alonzo Pinzon was a good captain. He would bring the *Pinta* back safely.

However, bad luck seemed to be hounding them. Off Portugal, another storm blew up. This time the *Nina* was badly damaged. It became impossible to go on. Columbus had to stop in Portugal for repairs.

When King John heard of his arrival, he invited Columbus to court. Too late, the king realized his mistake. "I should have helped you," he said to the admiral. "Then your discoveries would have belonged to Portugal."

Afterward, Columbus hurriedly boarded the *Nina*. He was afraid King John might take him prisoner. He might send a Portuguese fleet to the New World and steal Columbus's islands. Quickly, Columbus ordered the anchor to be lifted. He flew into the Atlantic. Then he sped south along the coast of Portugal. Finally, he entered the safety of Spanish waters in the Gulf of Cadiz.

Then another fear struck him. He worried that
Martin Alonzo Pinzon might have already arrived in
the *Pinta*. What if Martin Alonzo beat him back to the
Spanish court? What if he was claiming to be the real
hero of the voyage? Columbus was always generous
about praising others. At the same time, he wanted the
honors that were due to himself.

Arriving at Palos harbor, he scanned the docks
for the *Pinta*. To his relief, the ship was not there. He
had beaten the *Pinta* home.

But not by much. Scarcely had the *Nina*
anchored before the other ship came sailing in. The
citizens of Palos were astonished to see the ships. It
was hard to believe that Columbus had come back so
soon. His voyage was supposed to last a year. But the
trip to the New World and back took only thirty-two
weeks. People hailed Columbus as a genius. They
began calling him the "great navigator."

From Palos, Columbus traveled to the royal
court in Barcelona. Ferdinand and Isabella loaded
him with honors and titles. The weaver's son was
given the rank of a nobleman. From now on, he had
the right to call himself "admiral of the Great
Ocean." He also became "governor of the islands and
the mainland."

To Columbus, these titles were very important.
They meant that he would be master of all the lands
he discovered. His plan was to return to Hispaniola
as soon as possible.

The news of his voyage quickly spread all over Europe. It caused great excitement. But not everyone admired Columbus. For example, at the Spanish court some of the noblemen were jealous. Once at a banquet, a guest insisted the voyage was not important. It was true that Columbus had crossed the ocean. But if not him, then another man would have done so. Columbus leaned over and picked up a hard-boiled egg from a dish. He dared the nobles at the table to make the egg stand upright. Everyone tried. But the egg kept rolling over.

Finally, the egg came back to Columbus. He cracked the large end. Of course, then it stood up easily. He glanced around at the guests. "Look, gentlemen," he said. "Now any of you can do it." He added, "The important person is the one who succeeds first."

Columbus's discoveries posed a fresh worry for Spain. Ferdinand and Isabella feared that Portugal might challenge Spain's right to the islands. What was to stop King John II from sending his ships to the New World? To solve this problem, Spain turned to Pope Alexander VI.

The outcome was a "Line of Demarcation." The pope drew a line on the map of the Atlantic Ocean. All land discovered east of the line would belong to Portugal. Everything west of the line belonged to Spain. That line gave Portugal the land that later became Brazil.

On October 13, 1493, Columbus departed on his second voyage. This expedition was huge. There were 17 ships and over 1,200 men.

Reaching the New World, Columbus hastened to Hispaniola to see the men he had left behind. To his horror, La Navidad was gone. The stockade was burned. Later he learned that some of his men had become bandits. They left the stockade to seek gold. Boldly, they attacked a tribe of Indians who were not peaceful. They were trailed back to La Navidad. Everyone was killed.

Columbus was very upset. Eventually, he built another settlement. The city that replaced La Navidad was Isabella, in Puerto Rico. It would be the first European city in the Americas.

In many ways, the second trip went badly. Columbus's men became more and more angry. They complained that he was unfair and bossy. Even the Indians turned nasty when he forced them to give up their gold. On the other hand, Columbus continued to explore. He discovered both Puerto Rico and Jamaica. The expedition returned to Spain on June 11, 1495.

If the second voyage seemed unpleasant, the third was even worse. In 1498, Columbus sailed south. He discovered Trinidad and the coast of South America. But returning to Hispaniola, he found many problems. A revolt broke out against him. Complaints were sent back to Spain. The king and

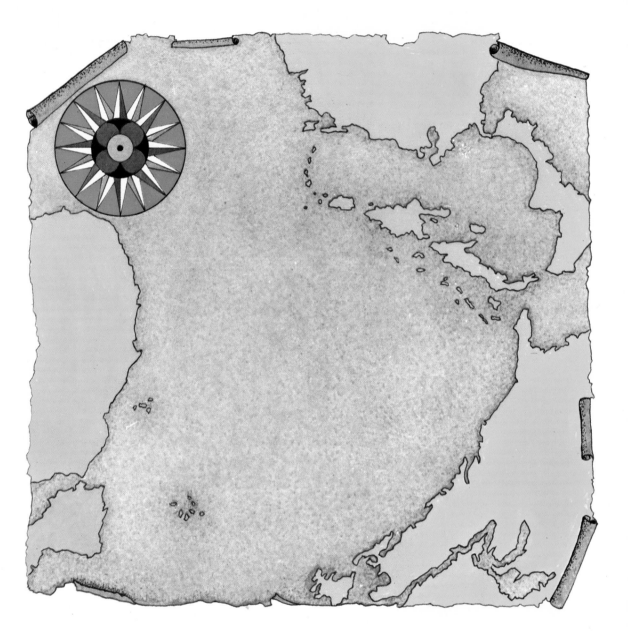

queen were displeased. They sent a governor all the
way to Hispaniola just to replace Columbus.

When the governor arrived, he arrested
Columbus. A prisoner now, Columbus was shipped
home in chains.

In Spain, the king and queen ordered his release. With sympathy, they listened to Columbus's side of the story. After all, his voyages had helped to win prestige for Spain. To show their gratitude, the king and queen agreed he could return to Hispaniola. But he did not get back all his old power.

Three years passed. The fourth voyage began on May 9, 1502. Columbus continued to lead the way in charting America. This time he went south, following along the coast of Central America. The lands he found are now Honduras, Nicaragua, Costa Rica, and Panama. Thanks to his discoveries, geographers were able to draw more accurate maps.

In May 1505, Columbus returned to Spain. By now his hardships were beginning to affect his health. He became ill. Yet he still planned another voyage. But when he reached the court, bad news was waiting. Queen Isabella, his protector, was dead. Columbus asked Ferdinand for permission to make another voyage. But the king refused.

This was Columbus's final disappointment. He died in Valladolid on May 20, 1506. He was fifty-five.

To the end of his life, he insisted he had landed in Asia. He thought the Caribbean islands were part of the East Indies. A fifth voyage, he believed, would have landed him on China's mainland.

Columbus never really understood what a grand feat he had accomplished. True—he had not sailed to China. Instead, he had discovered America!

The Admiral of the Great Ocean

In search of support for his "great enterprise," Christopher Columbus wrote to King Ferdinand of Spain. This letter, marked by faith and confidence, shows the courage of Columbus in offering to prove that he could reach Asia by sailing from the Occident ("onward to the East from the West"). This is part of what he said:

I have been a navigator since childhood. I have roamed the seas for many years. I have explored every part of the known world and have spoken with many: with religious, with seculars, with people of every faith, with Latins, Greeks, and Moors. I have acquired a knowledge of navigation, astronomy, and geometry; I am an expert cartographer who can draw up a map of the world. I can show the location of cities, rivers, mountains, and all manner of places as they really are. I have studied cosmography, history, and philosophy. I am certain I can reach the Indies, and I respectfully request Your Majesty to approve my enterprise. If Your Highness will grant me the means to execute my plans, no obstacle will stop me from making a success of this enterprise.

In April 1492, Ferdinand was convinced of the merit of Columbus's plan and approved it. In less than three months, Columbus managed to equip three ships: the *Nina,* the *Pinta,* and the *Santa Maria.* Columbus sailed from Palos on August 3, 1492, on his immortal enterprise, with the title "admiral of the Great Ocean."

Model of the flagship of the expedition of Christopher Columbus: the *Santa Maria*. The model is in the Historical Naval Museum of Venice. The original is in Vienna.

The Discovery of the "Indies"

Christopher Columbus did not know that he had discovered a new world. He firmly believed that he had found the shortest route to the land of gold, to those Indies that Marco Polo had described in his marvelous diaries. In fact, this is why Columbus called the natives "Indians," the peaceful people of the islands he discovered. He loved the natural beauty of these lands. He claimed them in the name of the Cross and of the king of Spain. Here is part of a letter to the Spanish monarch in which he describes Haiti (which he called Hispaniola):

All the islands are fertile, but this one is the measure by which they may be judged. The coastline has harbors superior to many I have seen in Europe, and there are great rivers on the island. The land is high and there are some spectacular mountain chains, taller than those of Tenerife. And everything is beautiful, lush, and fertile. There are hundreds of varieties of trees, some so high they seem to touch the sky. There are seven or eight varieties of palms alone, stunning in their beauty, and many evergreens. There are thousands of herbs and plants. I have seen an extraordinary number of pines and broad fields of cultivated crops. There are honey and many types of birds and fruit. In the interior of the island, there must be mines to account for the metals that the inhabitants of the place use.

After his discovery of America, Columbus made three more voyages of exploration. They are outlined on the map below. In September of 1493, he discovered Puerto Rico and Jamaica. In 1498, his third voyage brought him to Trinidad and the coast of South America, near the mouth of the Orinoco River. On his fourth voyage, in 1502, he discovered Central America and explored along the isthmus (Panama).

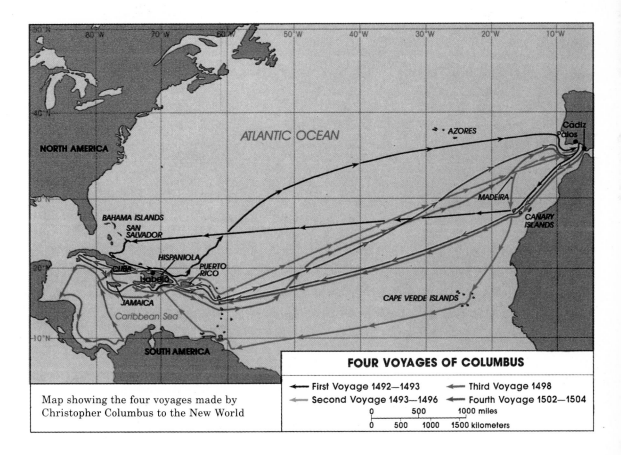

Map showing the four voyages made by Christopher Columbus to the New World

FOUR VOYAGES OF COLUMBUS

First Voyage 1492—1493   Third Voyage 1498
Second Voyage 1493—1496   Fourth Voyage 1502—1504

0   500   1000 miles
0   500   1000   1500 kilometers

Anecdotes About Christopher Columbus

I — The Coat of Arms of the Viceroy. As a boy, Columbus lived for awhile in the city of Siena, near the Church of Fontegiusta. It was at this time that he saw a girl in this church with whom he fell in love. Her wealthy family opposed the relationship since Columbus came from a modest family. The last time he saw his first love, believing he would have a glorious future, she said to him: "Send me news of your adventures." The news was long in coming, but after many years there arrived at the church a votive gift from the admiral of the Great Ocean: the coat of arms of Columbus as viceroy of Spain in the New World he had discovered.

That coat of arms was placed in the Church of Fontegiusta. The girl he had once met in that church recognized the name of Christopher Columbus.

II — The Eclipse in Jamaica. In need of food and fresh water, Columbus was once forced to drop anchor at Jamaica. But the natives there were extremely hostile.

Realizing that there was to be a lunar eclipse that night, Columbus spoke to them in these terms: "I am not hostile to you. All I want is food and water for my men. Let me have them. If you refuse, I will put out the moon and that will be the beginning of many misfortunes for you and your island." The natives opposed the admiral of the Great Ocean. But when they saw the moon vanish in the night sky, they fell on their knees. Trembling, they let Columbus have what he needed to continue his voyage.

Antique print illustrating the story, concerning Christopher Columbus, famous as "the egg of Columbus." The story, for which there is no real proof, is described in this book (page 82).

"We Give You Forever"

The king of Spain had to obtain the pope's permission to accept jurisdiction over the lands Columbus discovered. Here is part of the papal bull, addressed to King Ferdinand, giving Columbus the right to take these lands for Spain:

We know well that you intended to search for and to find islands and remote lands, both known and unknown, and to bring the inhabitants to the Catholic faith, and that you have not had time to complete so holy and benevolent a work. We know, finally, that to achieve this you invited our well-loved son, Christopher Columbus—a man certainly worthy of responsibility for such an enterprise—to go with ships and men, not without great fatigue and danger, to discover lands and remote islands and to sail into seas never navigated before...

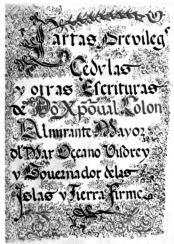

I see in particular the scope of this achievement, and of the spreading of the Christian faith...and I recognize that under the guidance of divine providence lands and islands are being found, and their inhabitants led into the Catholic faith.

And considering the importance of this work, freely and without any other motive, through our own initiative, by our generosity, and our apostolic authority, we

give to you forever and to your successors (King of Castile and of Leon), through the authority of God omnipotent and our gift, all the islands and the lands, discovered and to be discovered, known and unknown, in the Occident, limited by a line traced from the Arctic Pole to the Antartic Pole.

We command you to send to these lands and islands just men, moved by fear of God, expert in instructing the inhabitants in the Catholic faith and educating them in moral behavior.

Text of the privileges bestowed on Christopher Columbus by King Ferdinand and Queen Isabella

In his turn, the king, to the eternal glory of Columbus, gave the Great Navigator a heraldic coat of arms in which the castle of Castile and the lion of Leon occupied the two upper quarters. The two lower quarters showed islands in the midst of an ocean and five anchors representing the voyages of the admiral of the Great Ocean. The opposite side of the coat of arms bore the words in Spanish:

Por Castilla y por Leon — Nuevo Mondo hallo Colon

Translated, this means: Columbus discovered a new world for the glory of the sovereigns of Castile (the castle of Isabella) and Aragon (the lion of Ferdinand).

HISTORICAL CHRONOLOGY

Life of Columbus	Historical and Cultural Events
	1446 Death of Filippo Brunelleschi, leading Renaissance artist.
	1450 Johann Gutenberg perfects printing with movable type.
1451 Born in Genoa, exact date unknown.	
	1452 Birth of Leonardo da Vinci.

House where Columbus spent his childhood in Genoa; restored in 1700

Joan of Arc on Horseback— medieval French miniature

Life of Columbus	Historical and Cultural Events
	1453 End of Hundred Years War between England and France, notable for leadership of Joan of Arc. Constantinople falls to the Turks.
	1455 Outbreak of Wars of the Roses, civil wars in England.
	1469 Isabella of Castile marries Ferdinand of Aragon, unifying Spain. Birth of Niccolo Machiavelli, political philosopher.

Silver crown of Isabella the Catholic—
fifteenth century

Life of Columbus	Historical and Cultural Events
1472 Sails to North Africa.	
1473 Sails to Greek island of Chios.	**1473** Birth of Copernicus, father of modern astronomy.
	1475 Printing of Ptolemy's *Guide to Geography,* which stimulates European exploration.
1476 In battle off Cape Saint Vincent, swims six miles to Portuguese coast with aid of floating oar.	

Benin culture—bronze figures in high relief forming a procession

Raphael—*Madonna of the Chair;* done on wood

Life of Columbus	Historical and Cultural Events
1477 Sails to Iceland.	
1478 Marries Filipa Perestrello.	
	1483 Birth of Raphael, one of the world's greatest artists.
1484 King John II of Portugal rejects his plan to reach the East Indies by sailing west across the Atlantic.	

Cape of Good Hope, discovered by Bartholomew Dias

Lorenzo the Magnificent—portrait by Georgio Vasari

Life of Columbus	Historical and Cultural Events
1485 Columbus goes to Spain.	**1485** End of Wars of the Roses with victory of Henry VII.
1486 Meets King Ferdinand and Queen Isabella.	**1486** Affonso d'Aveira, Portuguese explorer, travels up Niger River in West Africa.
1488 King John II rejects his plan again.	**1488** Bartholomew Dias, Portuguese sea captain, rounds Cape of Good Hope, opening a sea route to India.
1489 Columbus returns to Spain.	

Figure of Jesus; fresco in tempera
Leonardo da Vinci—*The Last Supper*

Treaty of Tordesillas between
Spain and Portugal—signed page

Life of Columbus	Historical and Cultural Events
1492 Ferdinand and Isabella approve his plan; he sails to America, lands on Guanahani (San Salvador), discovers Cuba and Hispaniola, loses the *Santa Maria*.	**1492** Death of Lorenzo the Magnificent, dictator of Florence.
1493 Returns to Spain aboard the *Nina* followed by the *Pinta;* receives a hero's welcome; departs on his second voyage during which he discovers Puerto Rico and Jamaica.	**1493** Papal bull places Demarcation Line on map of the world, dividing discovered and undiscovered lands between Spain and Portugal. Birth of Paracelsus, pioneer of modern chemistry.

Francis I on the Throne—French miniature of the period

Joanna the Mad—portrait by Michael Sittow—sixteenth century

Life of Columbus	Historical and Cultural Events
1494 Faces discontent among his men on Hispaniola but manages to control it.	**1494** Spain and Portugal agree to shift Demarcation Line farther west. Spain and France begin war for domination of Italy.
1495 Returns to Spain.	**1495** Leonardo da Vinci begins work on *The Last Supper*.
	1496 Joanna the Mad, daughter of Ferdinand and Isabella, marries Philip the Handsome of Austria, uniting Hapsburg lands with those of Spain.
	1497 John Cabot, venetian sea captain, sailing for England, reaches the coast of North America.

Pietá —sculpture by Michelangelo

Life of Columbus	Historical and Cultural Events
1498 Departs on his third voyage, during which he discovers Trinidad and South America.	**1498** Vasco da Gama, Portuguese sea captain, sails around the Cape of Good Hope to India.
1499 New governor sends Columbus back to Spain in chains; he is liberated and rewarded by Ferdinand and Isabella.	**1499** Michelangelo finishes his *Pietá* in Rome.
	1500 Pedro Cabral, Portuguese sea captain, discovers Brazil.

Andrea Palladio—entrance to
the Olympic Theater in Venice

Life of Columbus	Historical and Cultural Events
1502 Departs on his fourth voyage during which he discovers Central America.	
1504 Return to Spain ill and exhausted.	
	1505 Death of Ivan the Great, founder of modern Russia.
1506 Columbus dies in Valladolid.	

Pizarro and His Men Battle the Indians, print by T. de Bray

Henry VIII jousts in the presence of his wife, Catherine of Aragon—miniature

Life of Columbus	Historical and Cultural Events
	1507 Martin Waldseemüller, German geographer, names New World after Venetian explorer, Amerigo Vespucci: AMERICA.
	1517 Portuguese reach Canton by sea and sign commercial agreement between Portugal and China.
	1533 Francisco Pizarro, Spanish conqueror, executes Atahualpa, Inca king, and imposes Spanish rule on Peru.
	1536 Henry VIII executes Anne Boleyn, the woman for whom he broke with the Catholic Church.
	1547 Birth of Miguel de Cervantes, author of *Don Quixote*.

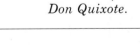

Miguel de Cervantes—*Don Quixote,* illustrated by G. Dore

WALLIS ELEMENTARY SCHOOL

BOOKS FOR FURTHER READING

Christopher Columbus by Lisl I. Weil, Atheneum, 1983.

Christopher Columbus: Admiral of the Sea by Mary P. Osborne, Dell, 1987.

Christopher Columbus on the Green Sea of Darkness by Gardner Soule, Watts, 1988.

Columbus and the Age of Exploration by Ken Stott, Watts, 1985.

Where Do You Think You're Going, Christopher Columbus? by Jean Fritz, Putnam, 1980.

INDEX